FUN WITH CHALK

KATE DAUBNEY
WITH PAUL VIRR

ARCTURUS

ARCTURUS

This edition published in 2018 by Arcturus Publishing Limited
26/27 Bickels Yard, 151–153 Bermondsey Street,
London SE1 3HA, UK

Copyright © Arcturus Holdings Limited

All rights reserved. No part of this publication may be reproduced, stored in a retrieval system, or transmitted, in any form or by any means, electronic, mechanical, photocopying, recording, or otherwise, without prior written permission in accordance with the provisions of the Copyright Act 1956 (as amended). Any person or persons who do any unauthorized act in relation to this publication may be liable to criminal prosecution and civil claims for damages.

Illustrated by Kate Daubney
Written by Paul Virr
Edited by Susannah Bailey
Designed by Square and Circus

ISBN: 978-1-78828-513-1
CH006109NT
Supplier 29 Date 0718 Print run 6807

Printed in China

DRAW WITH CHALK!

In this book you'll learn how to create lots of fun pictures—all with chalk! Below are the different ways that chalks are used in this book. If you're not sure how an effect is created, just come back to this page to find out.

Use the side of the chalk to create this effect.

Tap the chalk firmly to make chalk dust.

You can smudge or blend the chalk with your fingers!

Use the top edge of the chalk for a thin line.

Use the top flat edge of the chalk for a thick line.

Use the top edge of the chalk to make dots. This is called stippling.

LITTLE DUCKLING

Draw simple orange outlines, then fill with yellow strokes. Add ripples or splashes on the pond with white chalk.

Quack! Quack! Draw five small ducklings swimming on the pond.

PRETTY IN PINK

Start with bold pink shapes, then add details in black with the top edge of the chalk.

1

2

3

4

Draw more eye-catching pink flamingos, all standing on one leg!

Use white and pink chalk side-on to add reflections.

CUTE KOALAS

Layer white and black chalk, then smudge to get a fluffy effect!

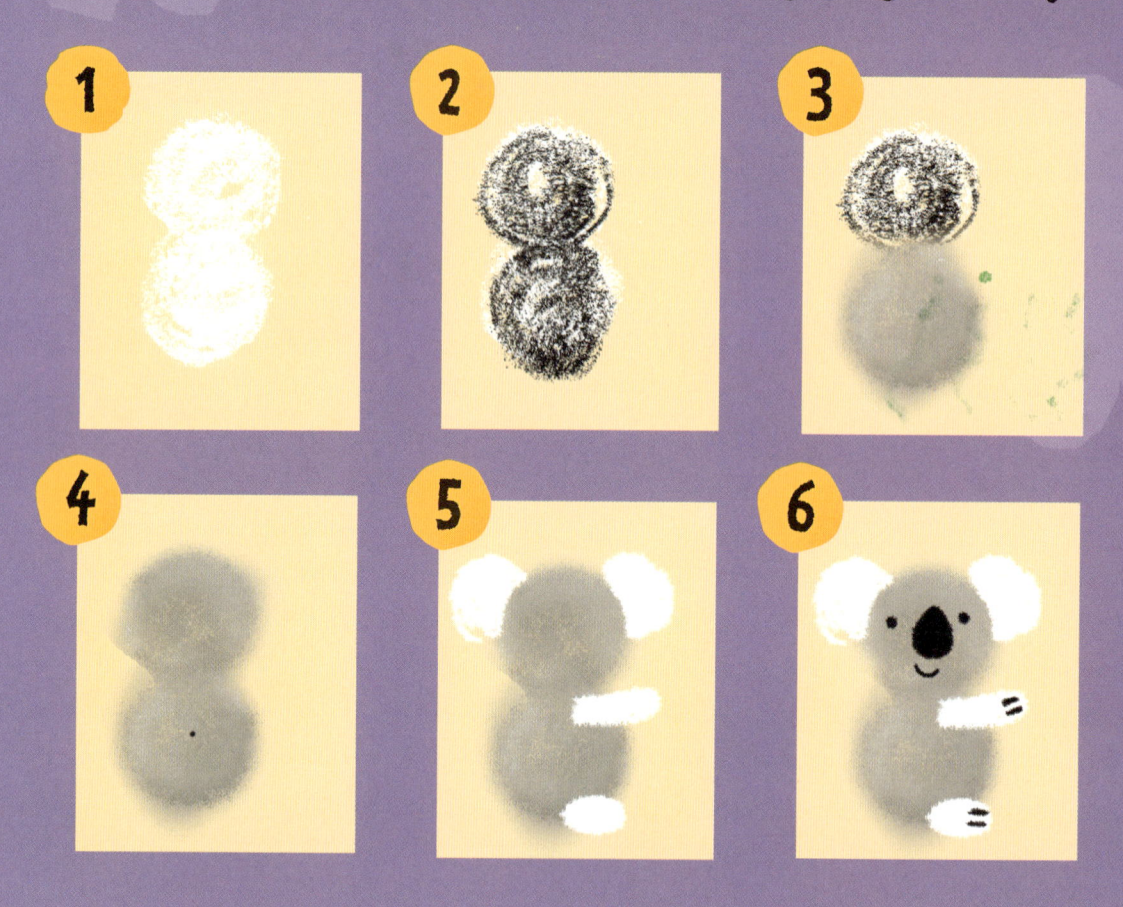

Now, make a cute baby koala.

Add more adorable koala bear friends to the tree.

JUMBO PARTY

Create patterns using spots, stripes, or shapes in different chalks.

Give each elephant at the party a fun pattern.

MONKEY MISCHIEF

Layer black and orange chalks, then blend with your fingers.

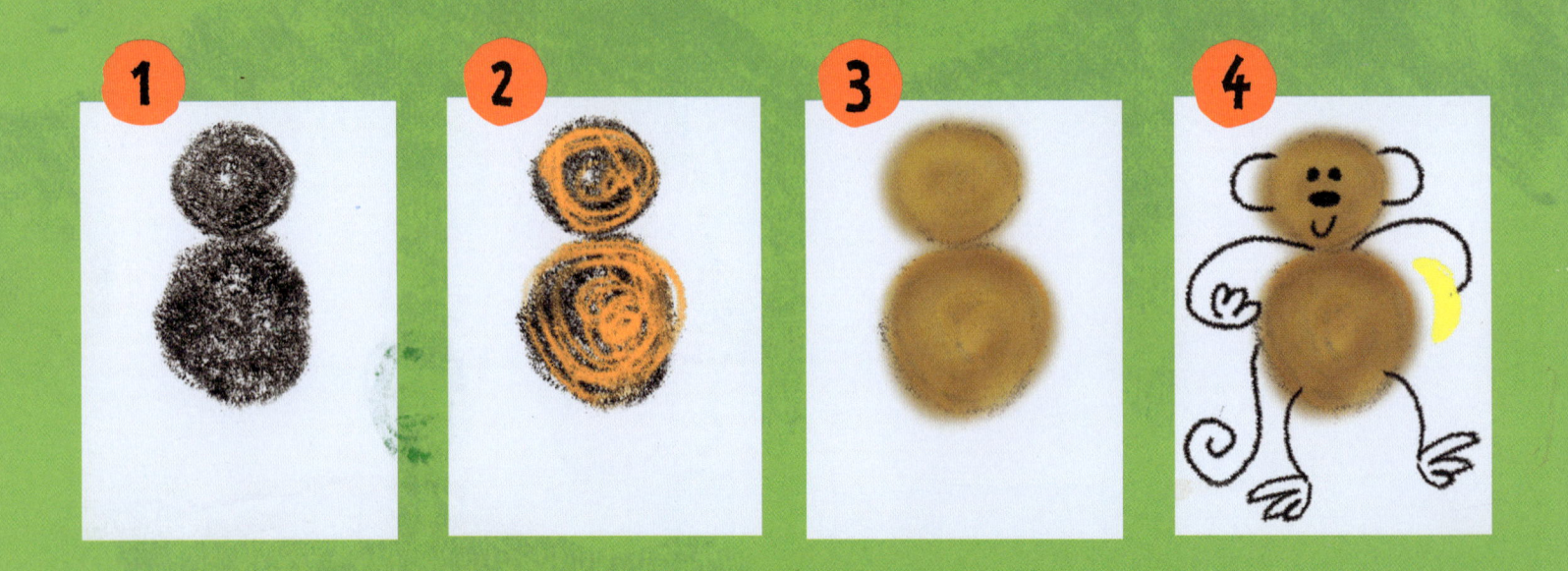

1 **2** **3** **4**

Can you make this swinging monkey?

1 **2** **3** **4**

12

Add more noisy monkeys, playing in the trees!

CRAZY CROCODILES

Draw simple outlines and fill them with different chalks. Then add curvy lines to give your crocodiles fun patterns!

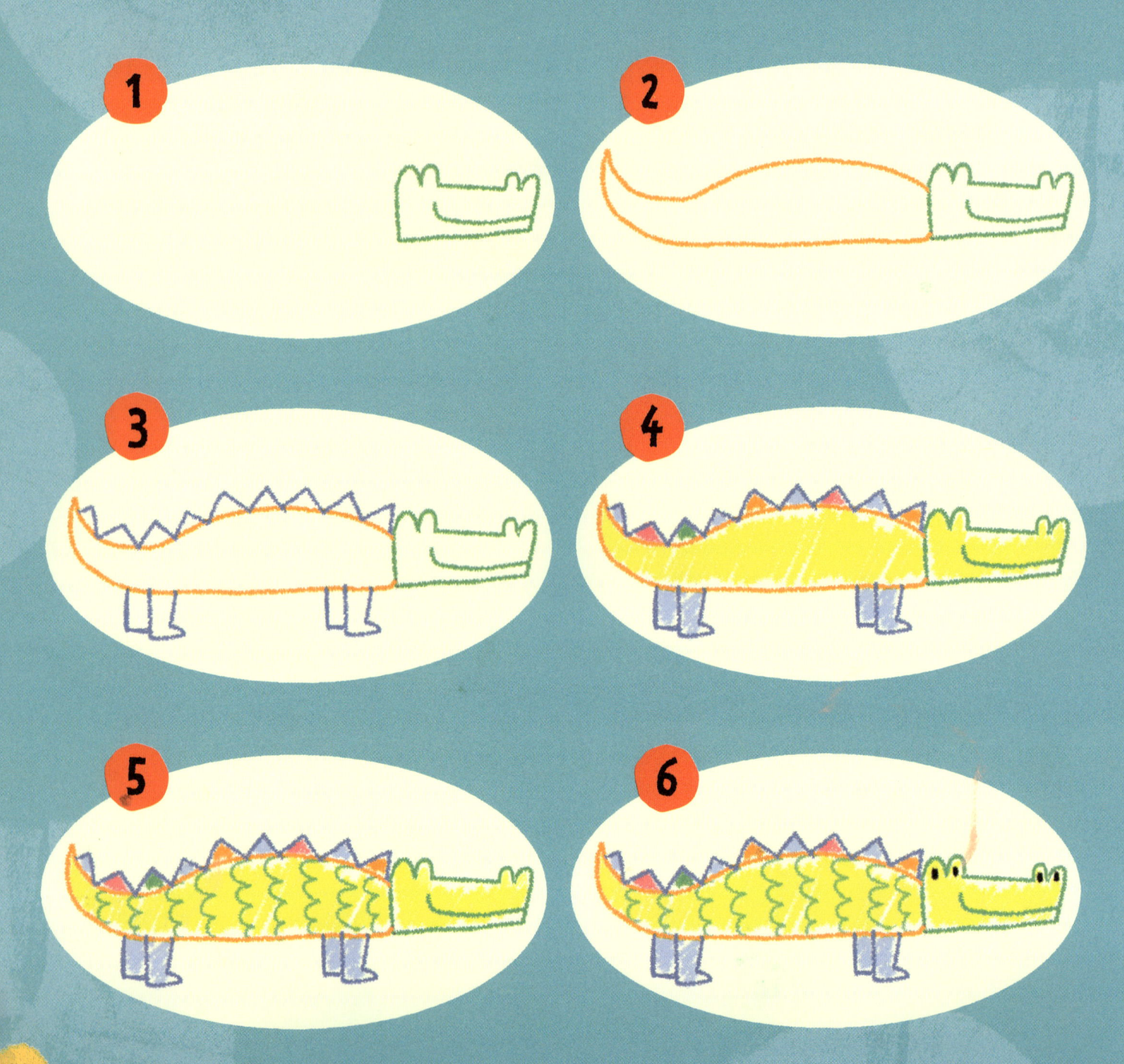

1
2
3
4
5
6

Add more snappy and happy crocodiles playing by the riverbank.

SiLLy SHEEP

Draw scribbly lines on top of white to make a fluffy sheep shape.

1

2

3

4

Add some sheep running about!

1

2

3

Draw more fluffy sheep for Alfie the sheepdog to round up!

17

CRAWLY CATERPILLARS

Use your chalks end-on, twisting to create circles. Then add legs and faces.

Or layer two chalks, smudging upward to make a hairy caterpillar!

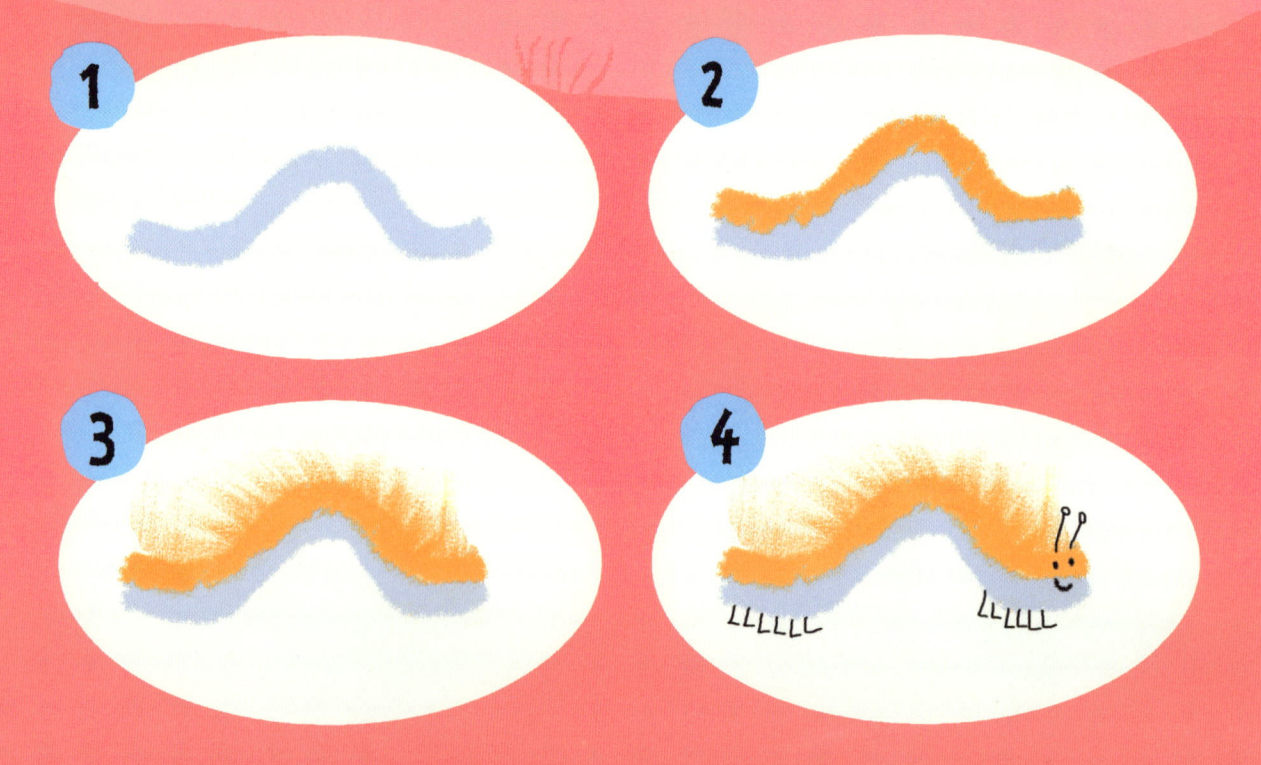

Add more crawly caterpillars, munching on their lunch!

GIGGLY GIRAFFES

Use different chalks to create patterns with squares, circles, and triangles.

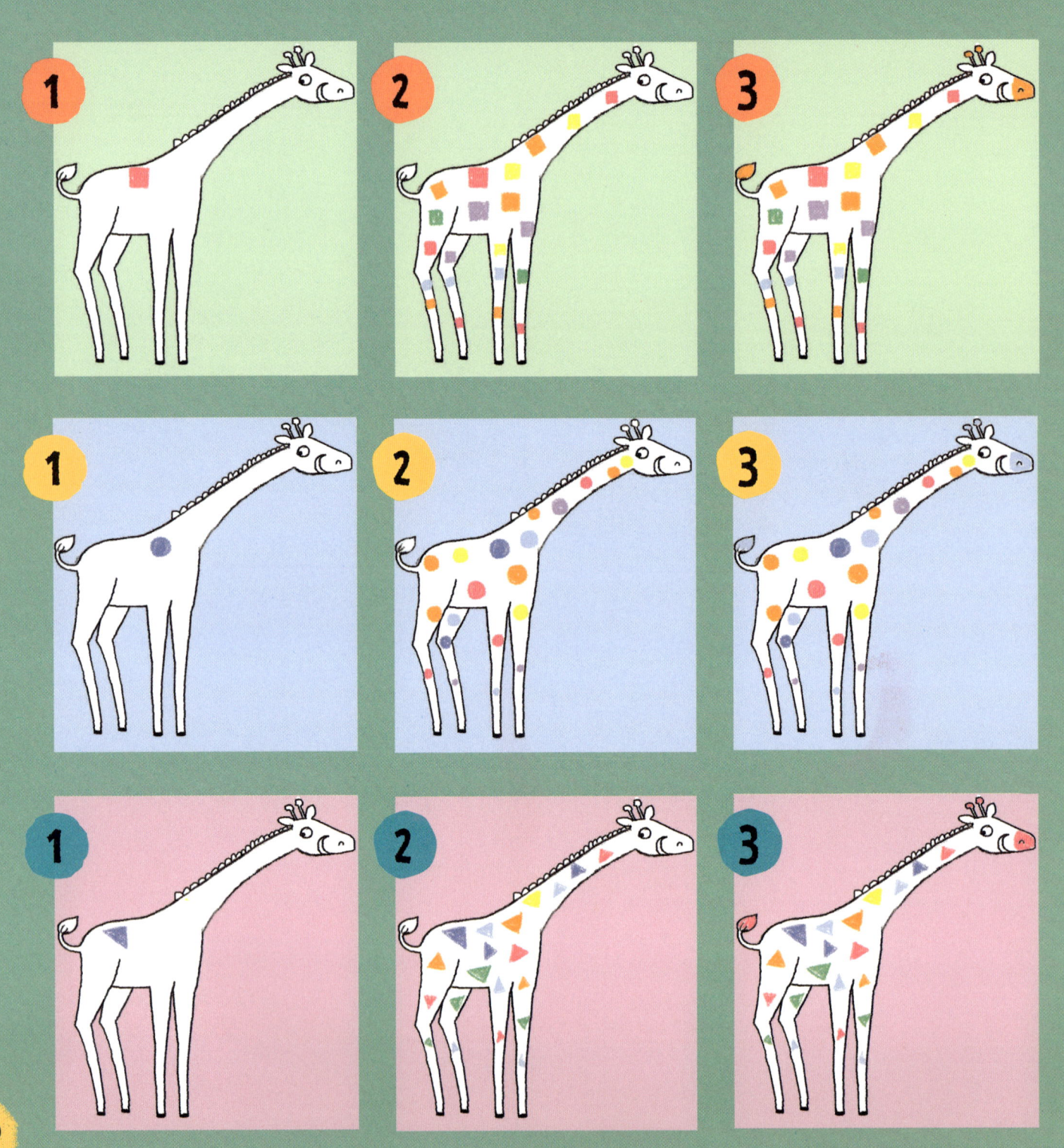

Give these ginormous giraffes some fun new patterns!

SWIRLY SNAILS

Draw a spiral on top of a circle shape. Add a body, eyes on stalks, and a smile!

1
2
3
4
5

Now, add more snails climbing to the top of the wall.

BEAUTIFUL BUTTERFLIES

Draw circles, spirals, or spots to decorate your butterflies.

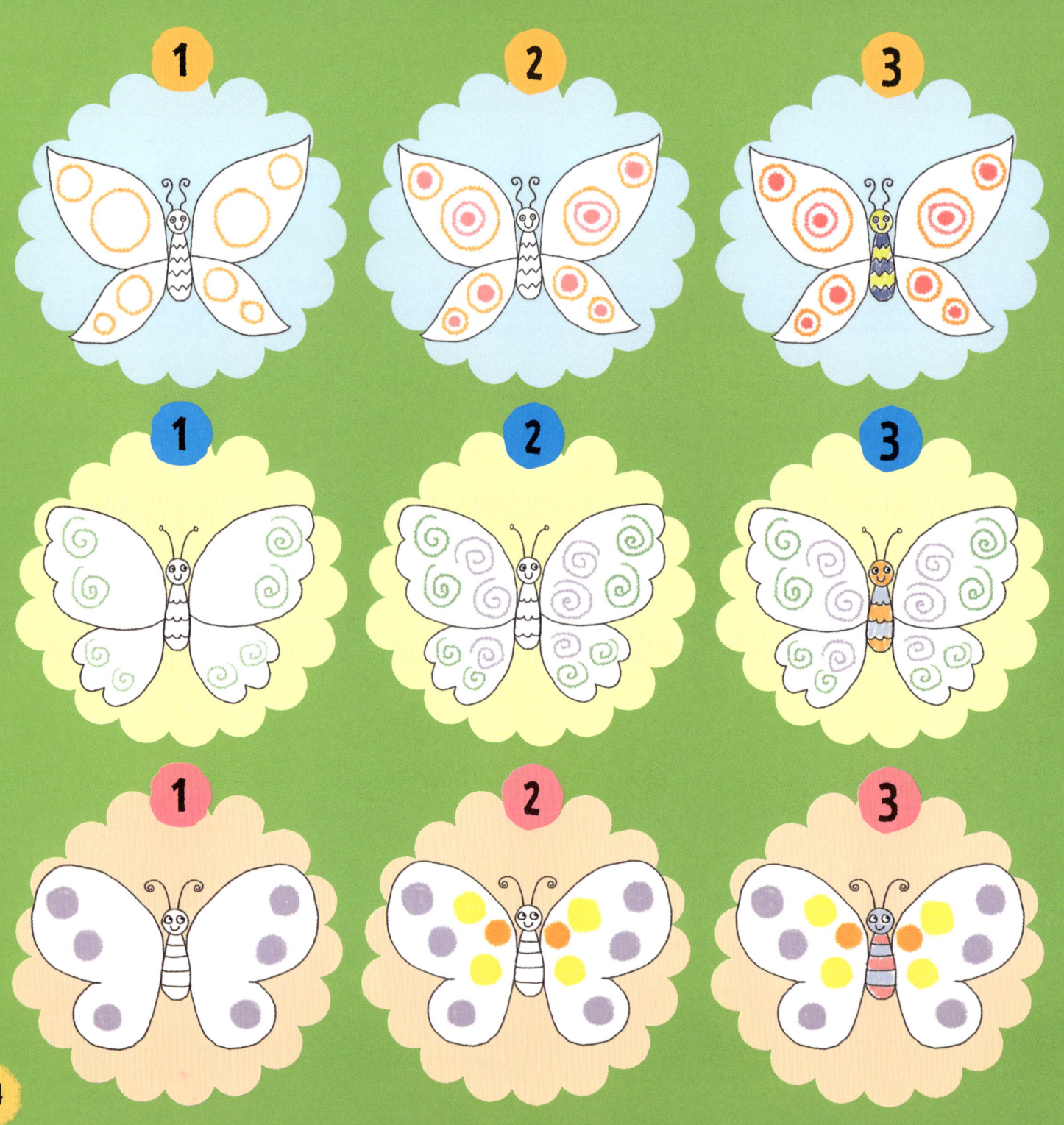

Add pretty patterns to these fluttery creatures.

CUDDLY TEDDY

Can you make this cute teddy bear?

1
2
3
4
5
6

Add more hungry bears to this picnic scene!

JIGGLY JELLYFISH

Blend rough ovals of different chalks. Add faces and curly tentacles.

Or start your jellyfish with half circles instead of ovals.

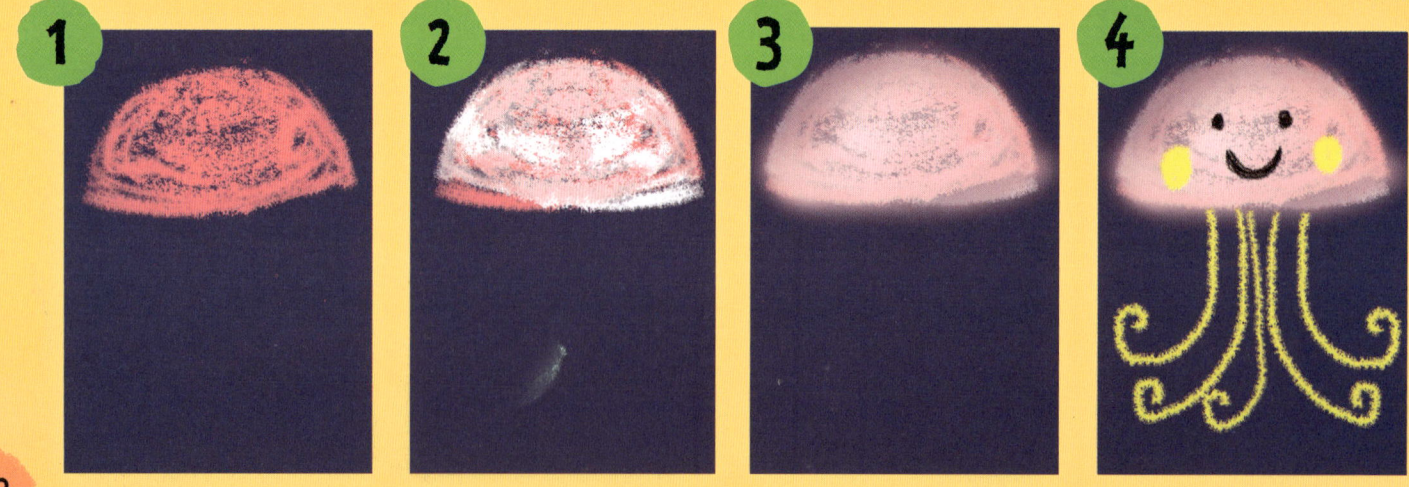

28

Dive in and draw more happy jellyfish bobbing along in the sea!

PLAYFUL PENGUINS

Start with two circle shapes for the head and body. Then add the details.

Dress up your penguins with hats and scarves to keep them warm!

Give these two penguins some friends
to play with in the snow! Then use the side of the chalk
to add ice to the lake.

WACKY WHALES

Fill a whale outline with chalk. Add flippers, a tail, a face, and a waterspout!

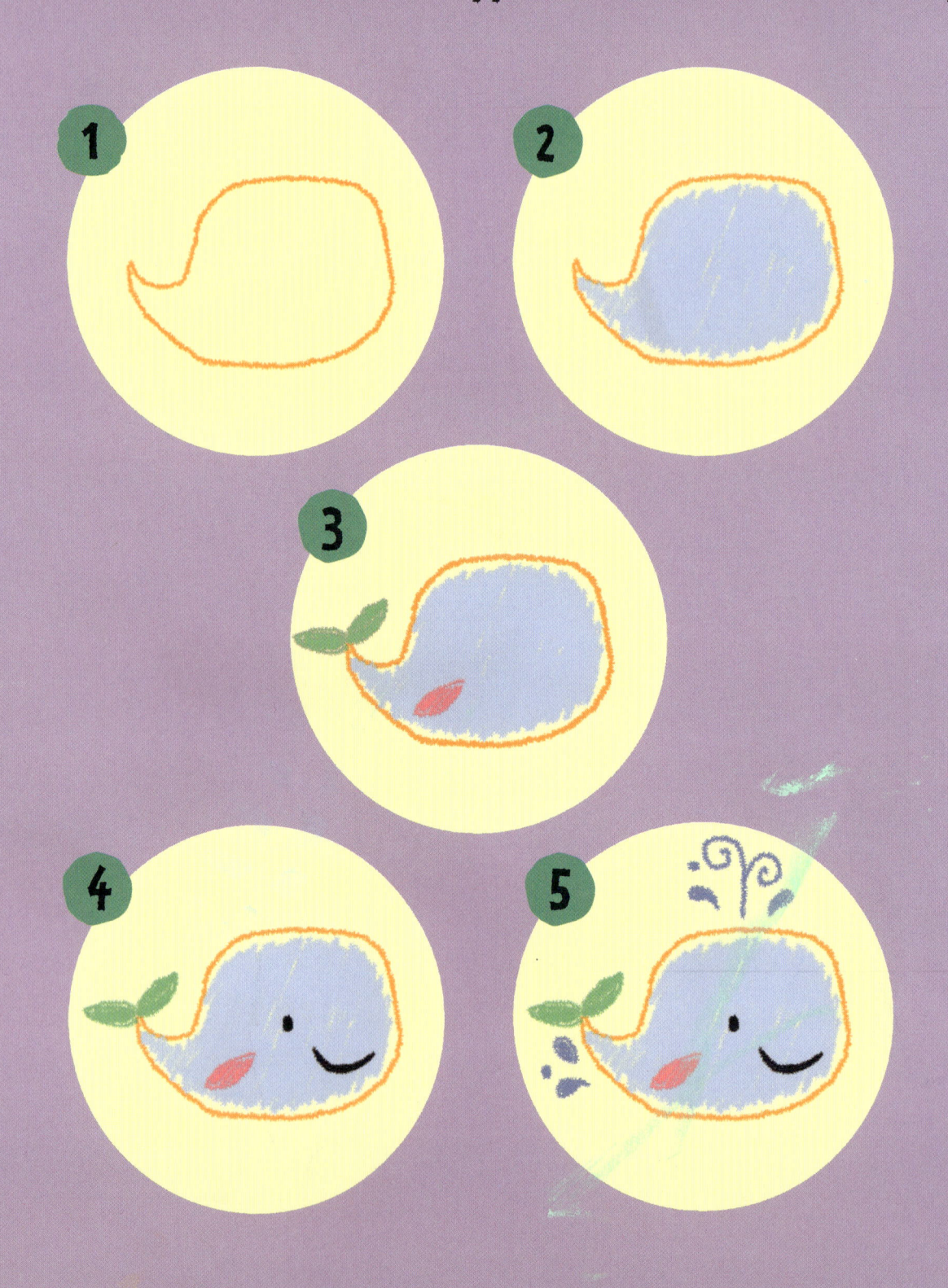

Draw some more whales (without waterspouts) playing in the sea!

SWIMMING SEAHORSES

Start with shapes for the head and body. Add the crest, tail, and fin, then finish off with a smiley face!

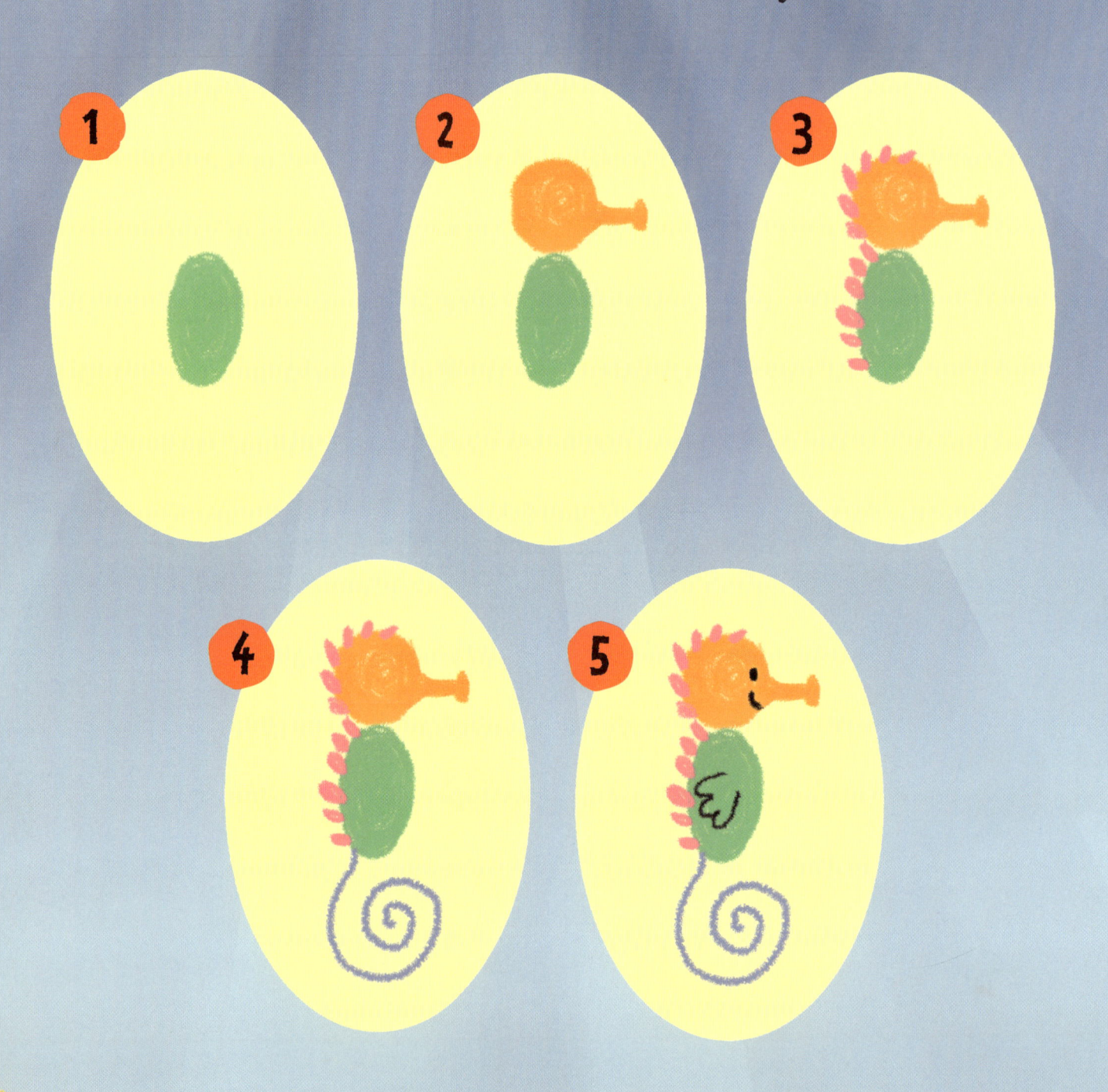

1
2
3
4
5

Add some seahorse friends to this undersea scene.
Use white chalk, end-on, to add bubbles, too.

35

DARTING DOLPHINS

Fill your dolphin outline with chalk, then add the details.

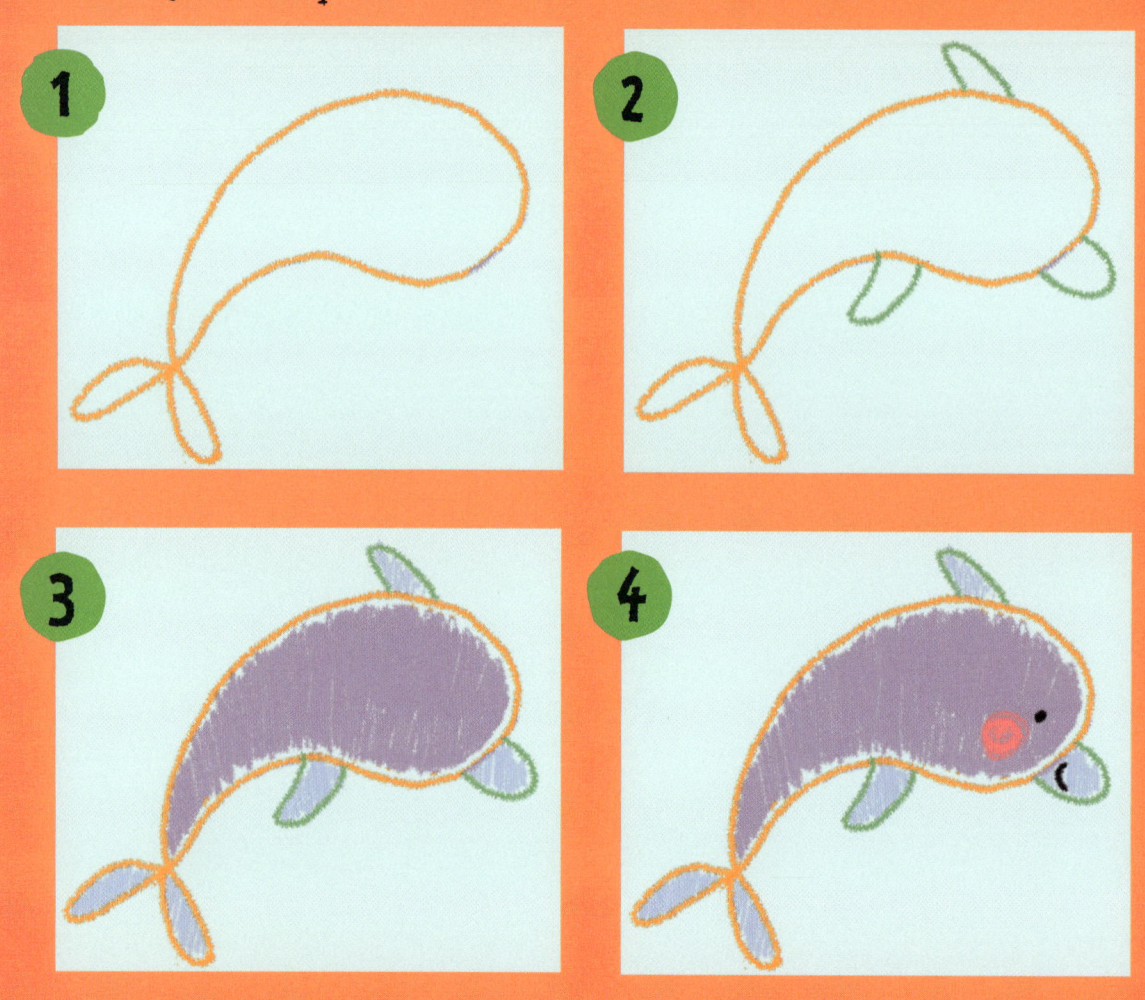

Give your dolphin some baby dolphins to swim alongside.

Add more playful dolphins, swimming through the waves.

FISHY FASHION

Use different chalks to add patterns to your fish. Smudge, blend—get creative!

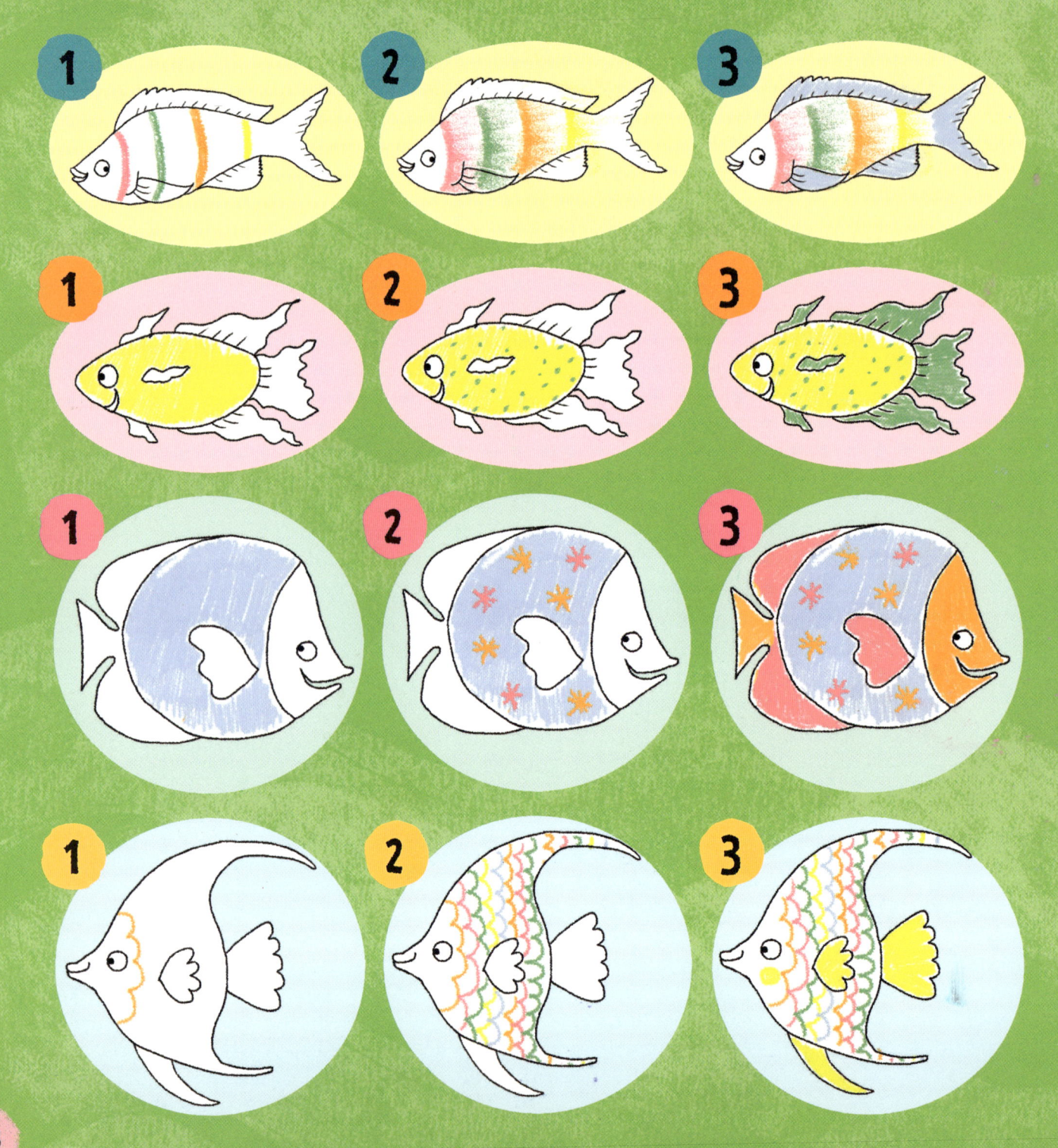

These fish need brightening up to match their coral reef home.

SURF CRAZY

Start your crab with an oval shape. Then add the frill, legs, eyes, and claws!

Use chalks end-on to create a lobster out of circles.

Surf's up! Add some crabs and lobsters
having fun down at the beach.

SUPER SUBMARINES

Outline your sub, then fill it with chalk. Add faces at the windows.

1

2

3

Add yourself and your friends here!

Dive! Dive! Add more submarines ready to explore the ocean depths.

Use white chalk, side-on, to add ocean currents.

STORMY CLOUDS

Layer black and white chalk to make dark clouds. Add dashes for rain and bold yellow zig-zags for lightning!

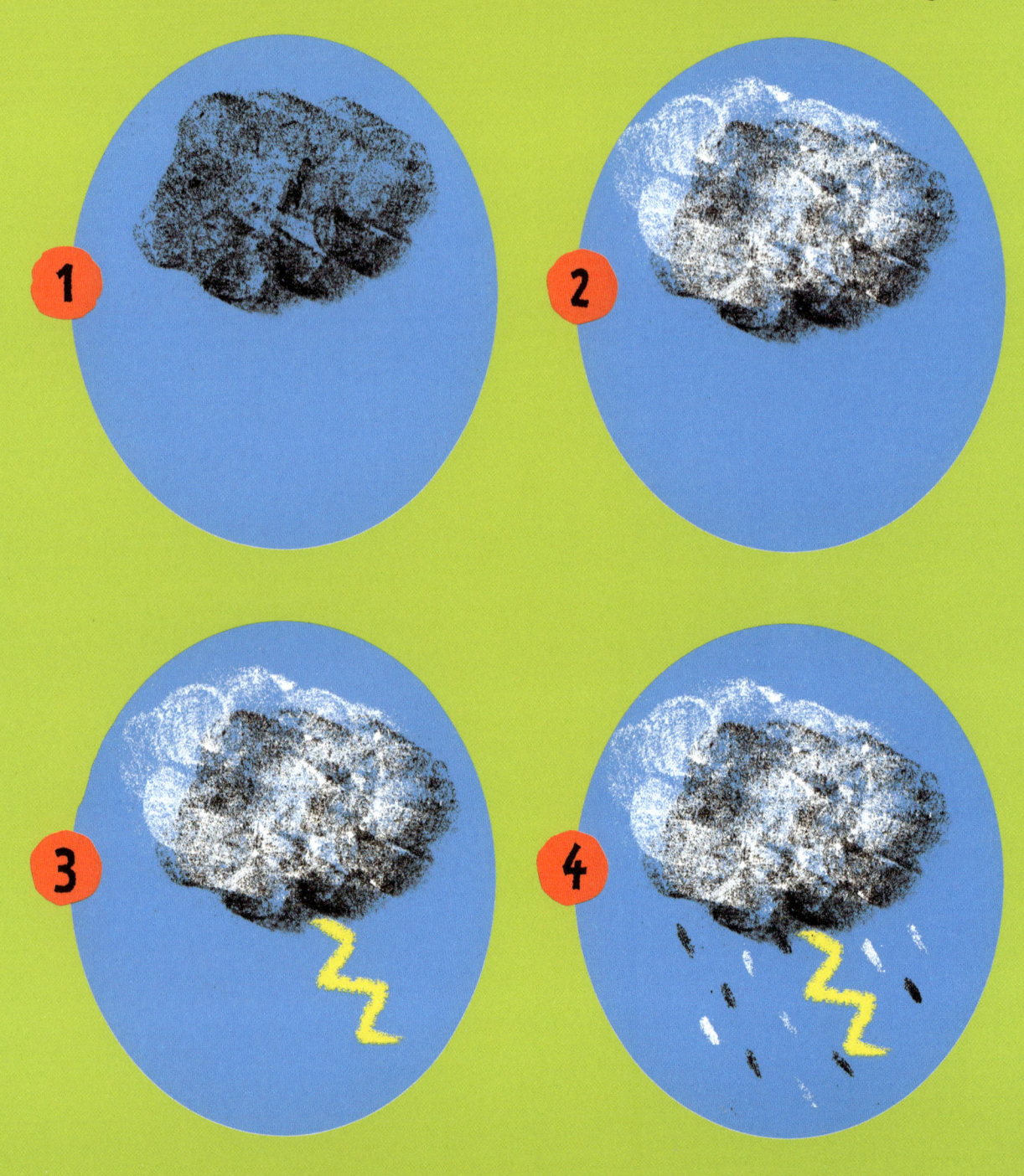

1

2

3

4

Hold on tight, it's going to be a stormy night!
Add more clouds, rain, and lightning!

Use white chalk, to add swirly waves.

UNDERSEA URCHINS

Use bold stripes to create your sea urchin body. Then, add spots with different chalks and smudge outward to make your urchin spiky!

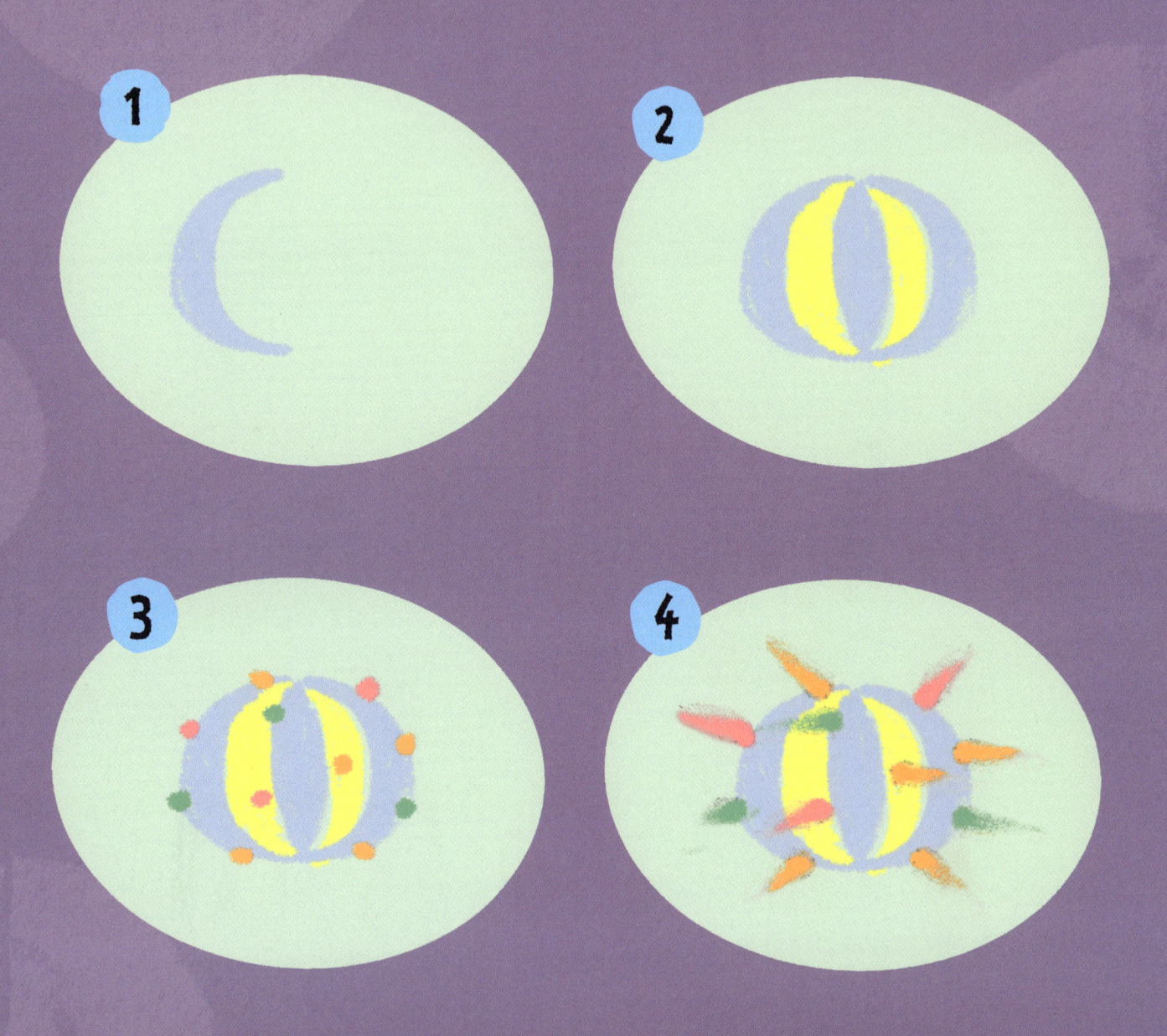

1
2
3
4

Who lives at the bottom of the deep, dark sea?
Add spiky sea urchins to this scene.

47

TOTALLY TURTLES

Start with three circles, then use different chalks to fill the rings and make patterns.

1
2
3
4
5
6

Add more turtles with patterned shells on the beach.

MAGICAL MERMAID

Start with the head and arms, by smudging white chalk over pink. Add the face and hair, then add a tail with a pattern of frilly lines.

1
2
3
4
5
6

Add more swimming mermaids to this undersea party!

BEAUTIFUL BALLOONS

Use bold stripes to make your balloon. Add a basket and ropes—ready to fly!

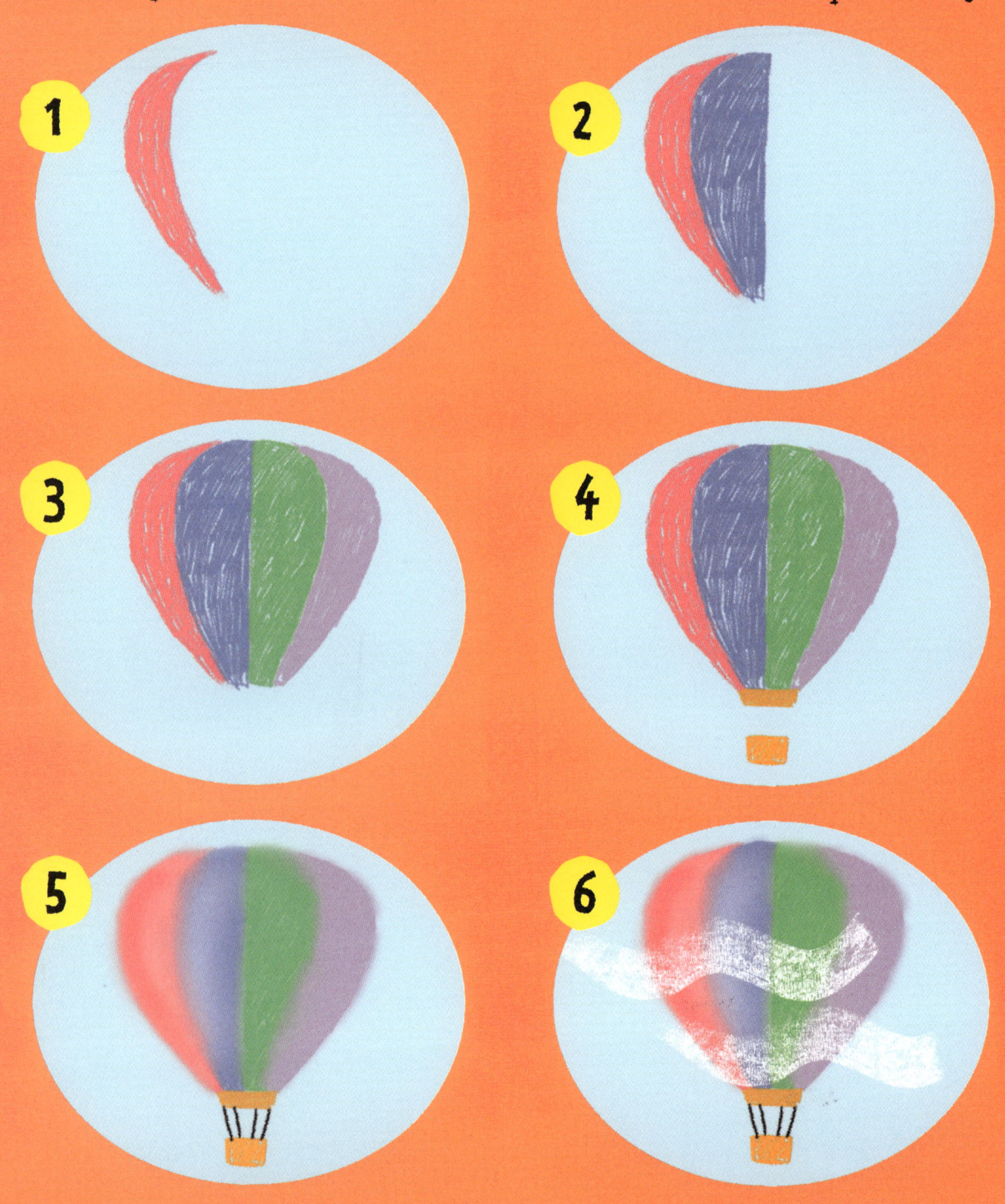

52

Fill the sky with amazing hot air balloons.

Use white chalk to add wisps of cloud.

MONSTER TRUCKS!

Add flames or other designs to your monster trucks. Smudge dark chalk around the wheels to make the mud fly!

Give these trucks totally awesome paint jobs!

BATTLE TIME

Add black, then add white on top. Blend them inward to get a metallic effect!

1 2 3

Use smudging to create shiny shields, then add pattern designs.

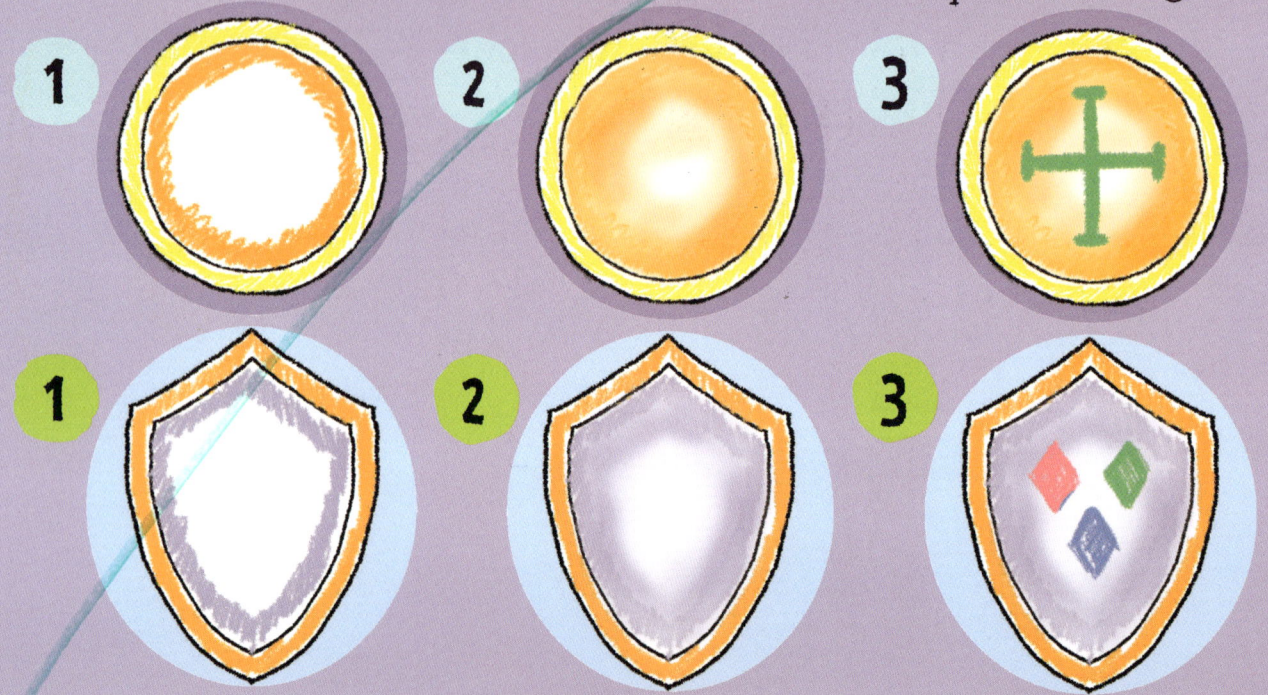

1 2 3

1 2 3

56

Use your chalks to dress these knights up so they are ready to face the dragon. Don't forget the shields!

STROLLING DINO

Join bold chalk shapes to make this Stegosaurus (STEG-oh-SORE-us).

1

2

3

4

5

6

Draw some roar-some dinosaurs with dazzlingly different chalk patterns.

HUNGRY DiNO

Add shapes for the body and head. Shade in stripes and blend up for the neck.

1
2
3
4
5
6

60

Draw a veggie dinosaur with a long neck to munch on this tree!

SPEEDY RACECARS!

Create your cars with solid chalk shapes. Smudge to create a high-speed effect.

1.
2.
3.
4.
5.
6.

62

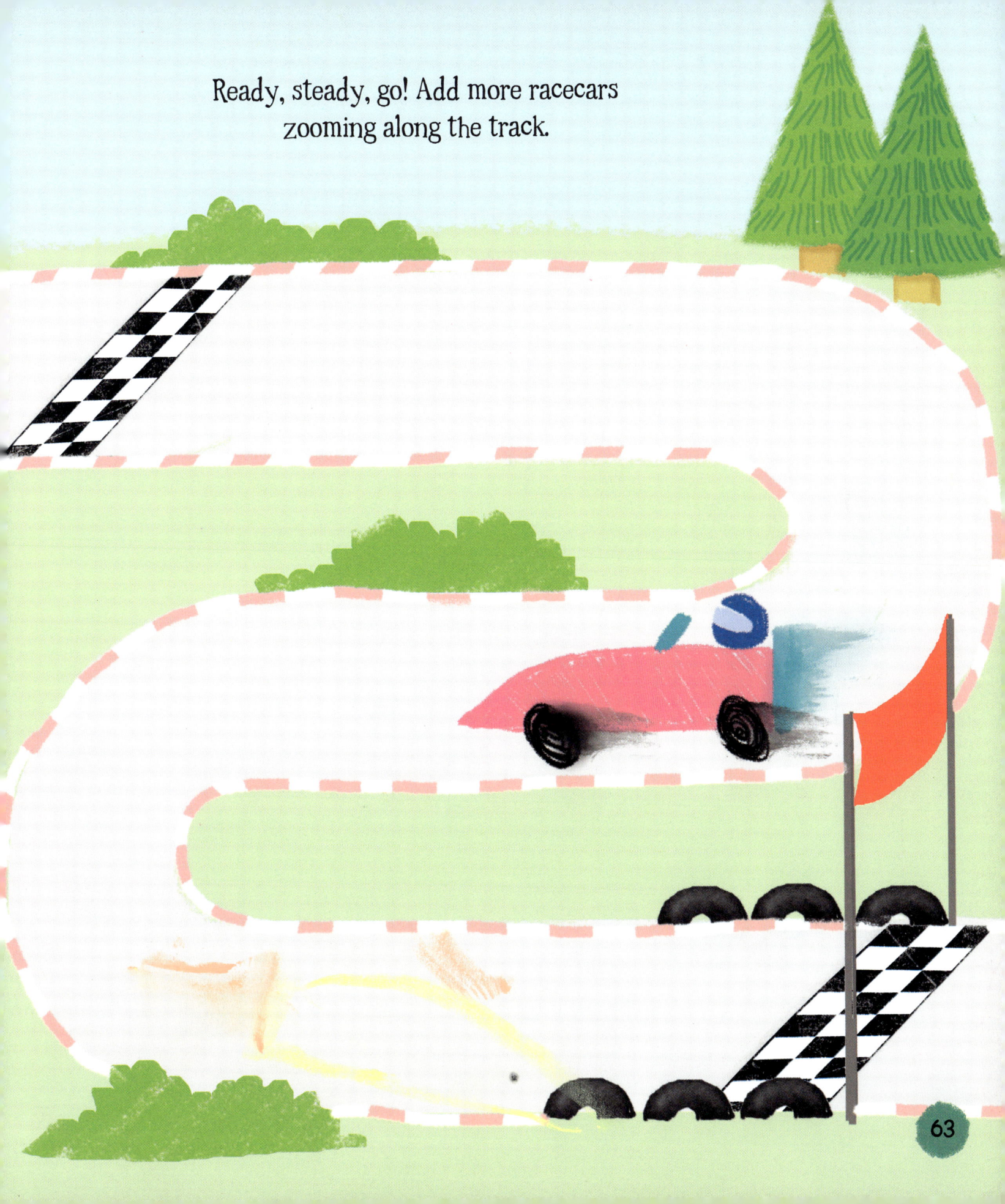

Ready, steady, go! Add more racecars zooming along the track.

ROBOT FACTORY

Use two rectangles or circles to create these awesome robots.

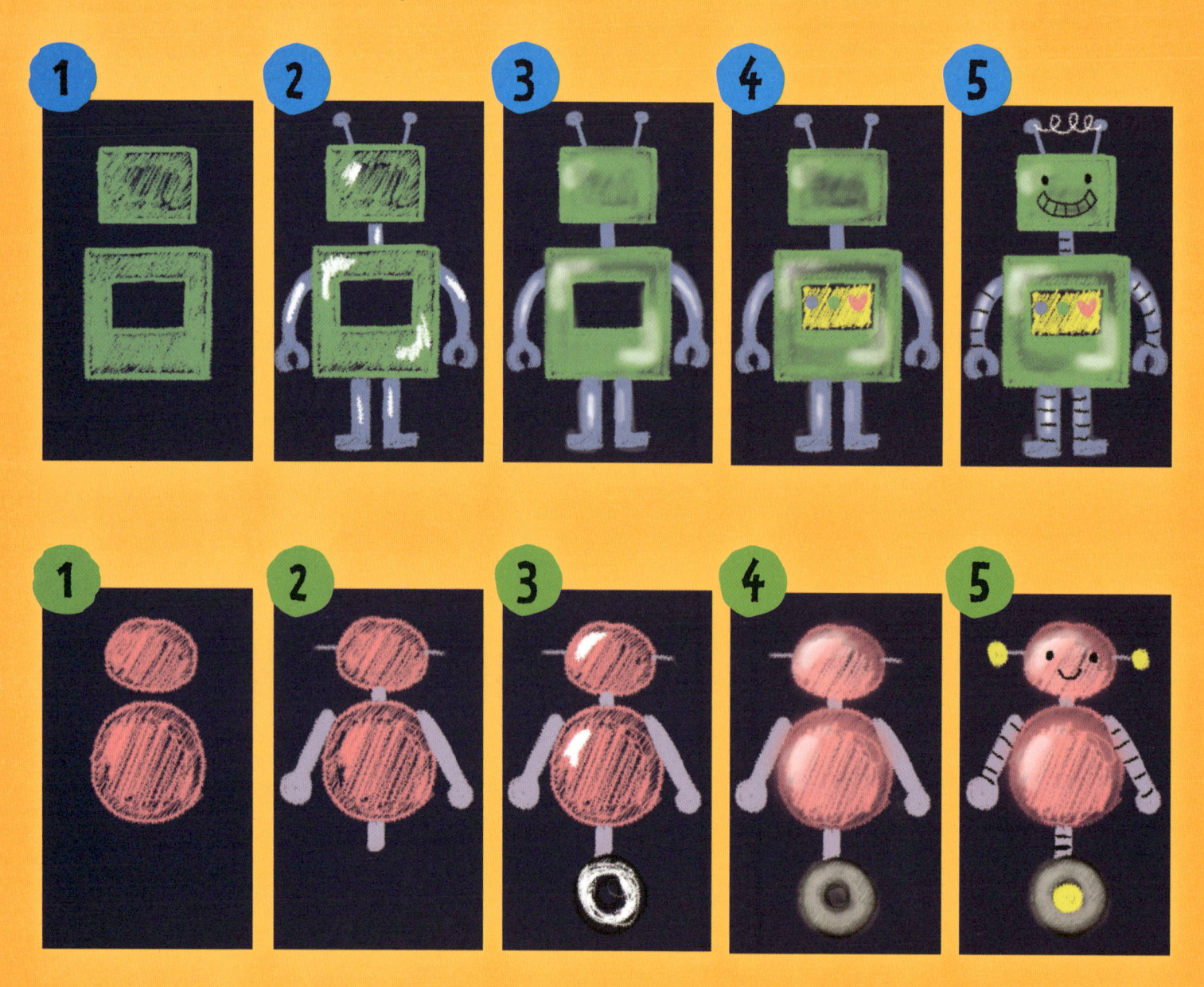

1 2 3 4 5

1 2 3 4 5

Add white over your chalk shading and smudge to create a metallic effect.

Get busy and build some shiny new robots now!

FARMYARD FUN

Create your tractor from simple shapes. Add wheels and details in black.

Layer scribbles of yellow and orange chalk, then blend to make hay.

66

Give the farmer a tractor to carry hay to her hungry animals. Add more hay too!

AMAZING ALIENS

Decorate your aliens with spots, stripes, or blended chalks.

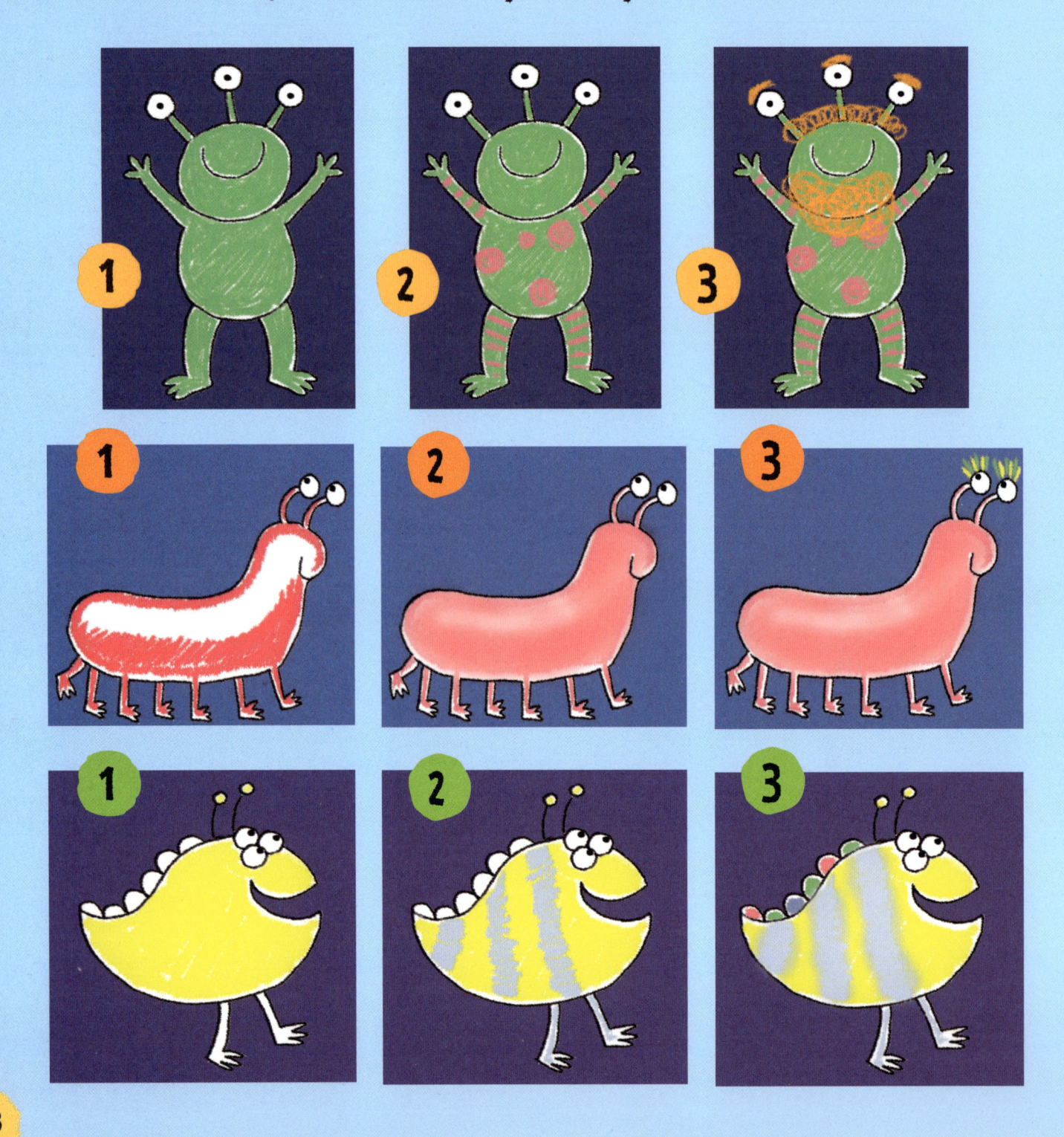

Give these aliens amazing designs that are simply out of this world!

3, 2, 1 ... BLAST OFF!

Create these spacecrafts with simple outlines. Fill in, then add details.

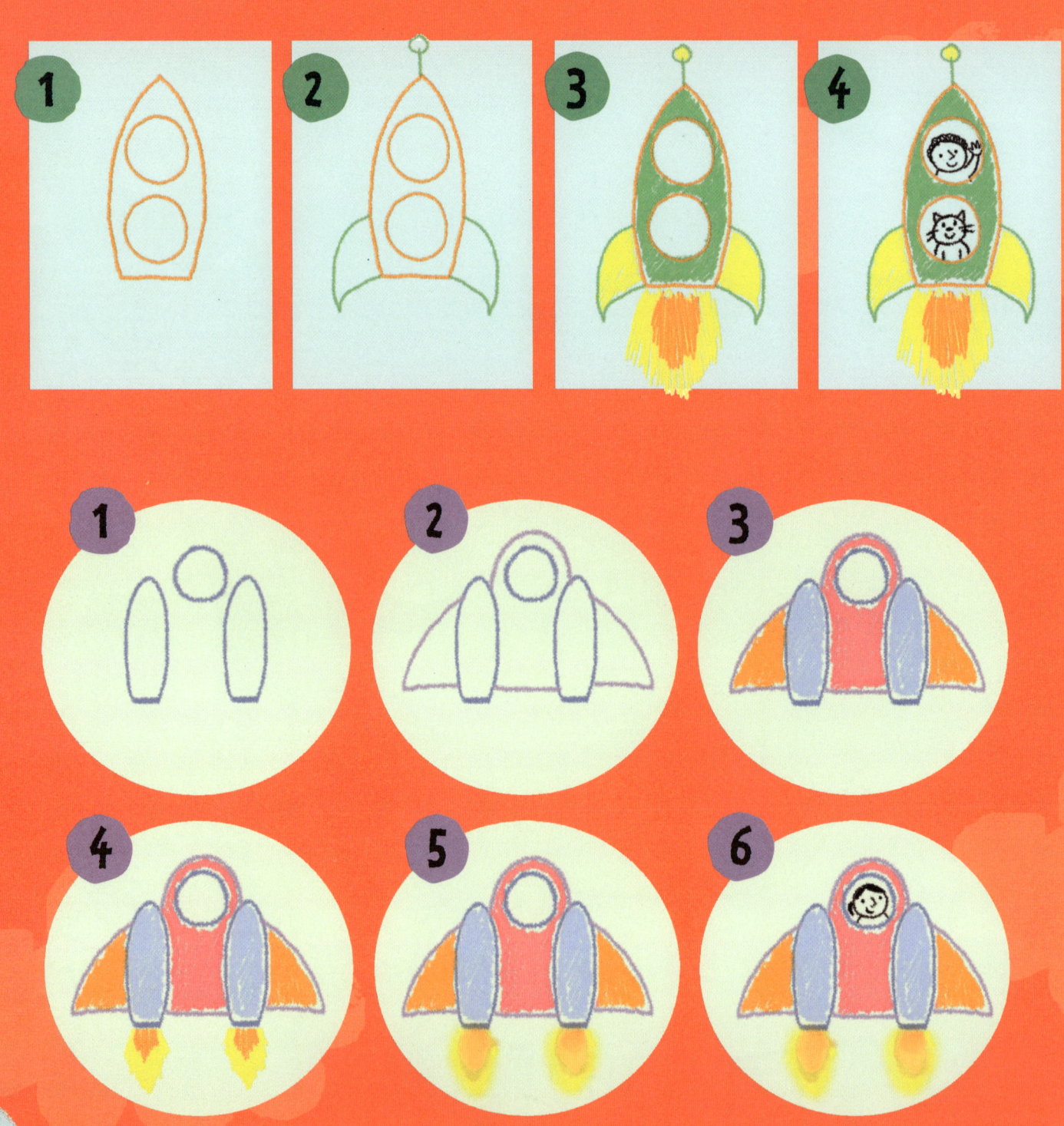

Draw your spacecraft here. Make sure to add flames shooting out at the bottom!

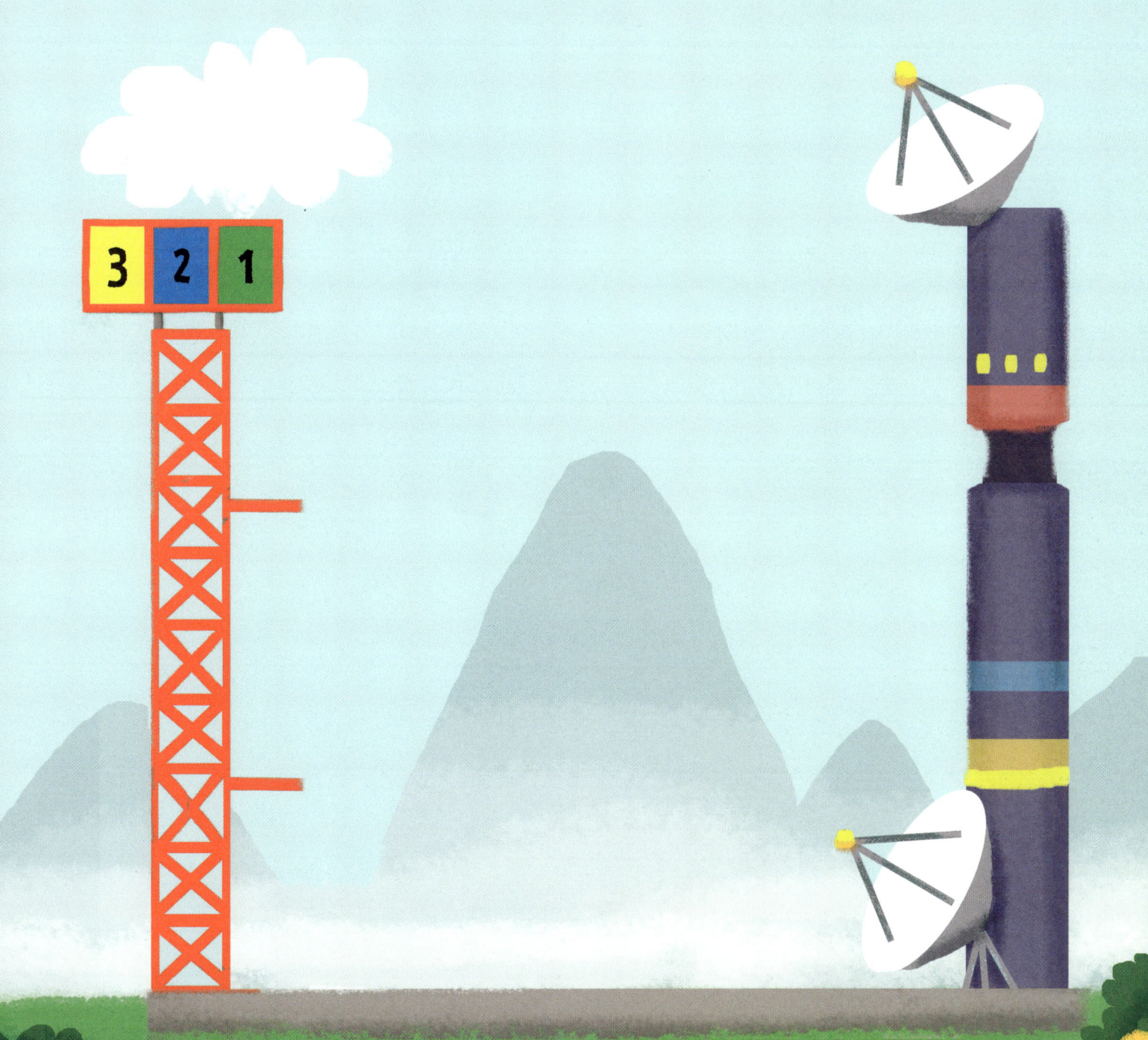

PIRATES AHOY!

Follow the steps to create a pirate captain and first mate for your ship.

This pirate ship needs a captain and first mate.
Draw them now, before the crew rebels!

BEACH MONSTERS

Scribble, blend, and draw to create some friendly monsters.

It's sunny, so don't forget to add sunglasses!

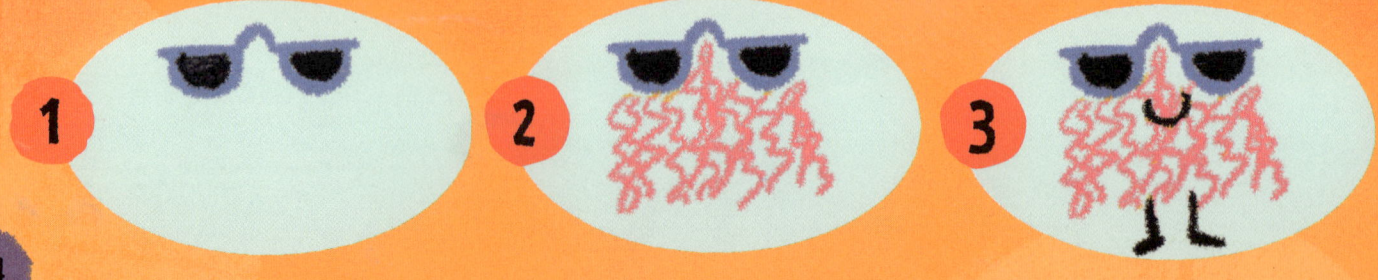

Add more monsters having fun on the beach.

SNOWY DAY FUN

Spin white chalk around side-on to create a snowman. Then dress him up!

Build a snowman, or use your white chalk end-on to add more snowballs!

BRIGHT KITES

Shade in triangles and squares with different chalks to create cool kites.

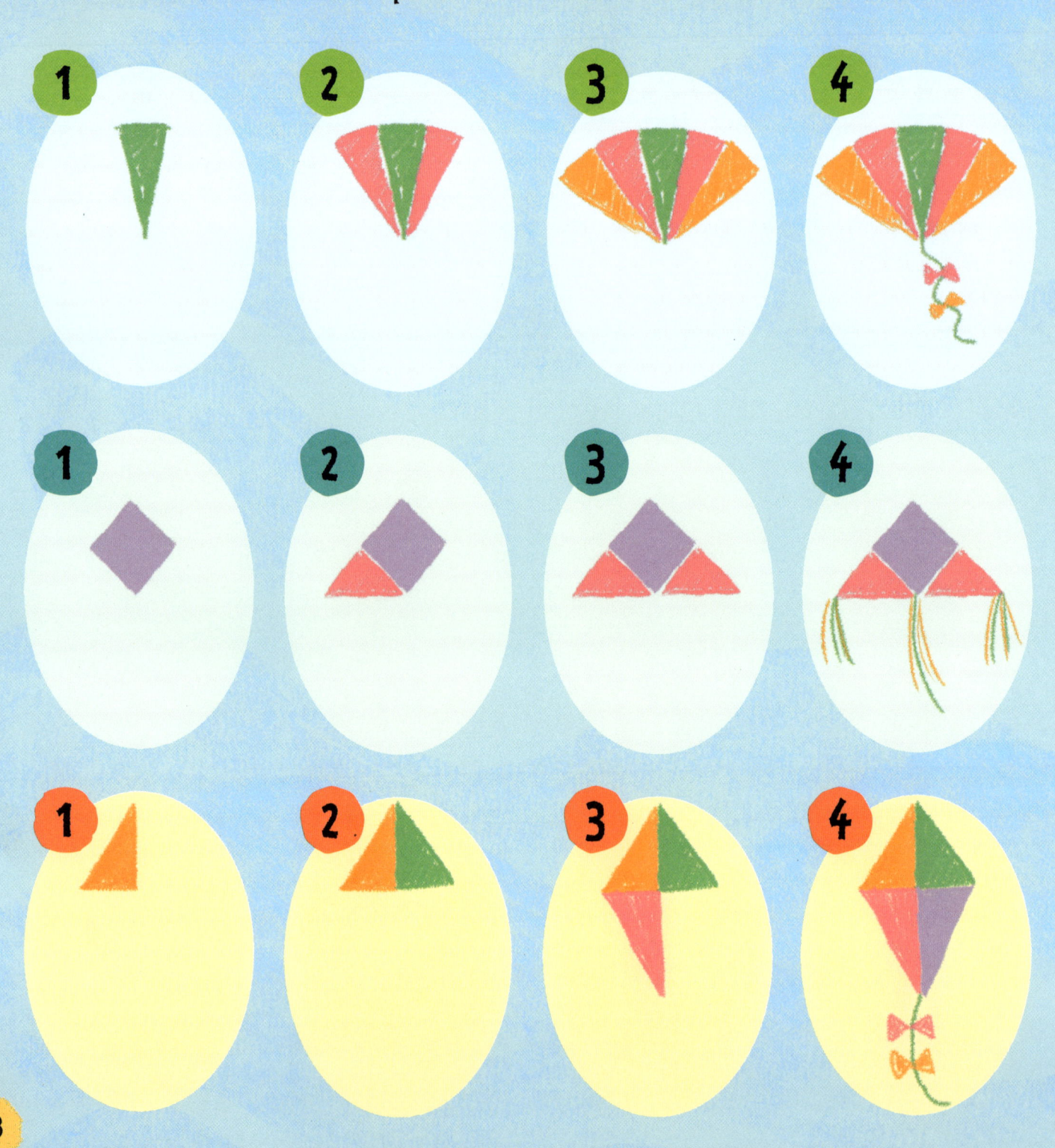

1 2 3 4

1 2 3 4

1 2 3 4

It's a breezy day. Give everyone a fun kite to fly.

FLOWER POWER

Draw, layer, and blend different chalks to create bright flowers.

These busy bees need more flowers. Add some now, so that they can make some honey.

PRETTY EASTER EGGS

Use stripes, spots, or a mix of patterns to decorate your eggs.

These yummy chocolate eggs need decorating!

SUPER SEASHELLS

Shade and blend to decorate your seashells.

Brighten up the beach by giving these seashells a makeover. Get really creative with the patterns!

SEASIDE SANDCASTLE

Use your chalks side-on, to create shapes for an eye-catching castle.

1
2
3
4
5
6

Now, build a sandcastle on the beach. Don't forget to add flags!

SANTA'S SLEIGH RIDE

Join simple shapes and blend in black to make a furry reindeer. Then add details.

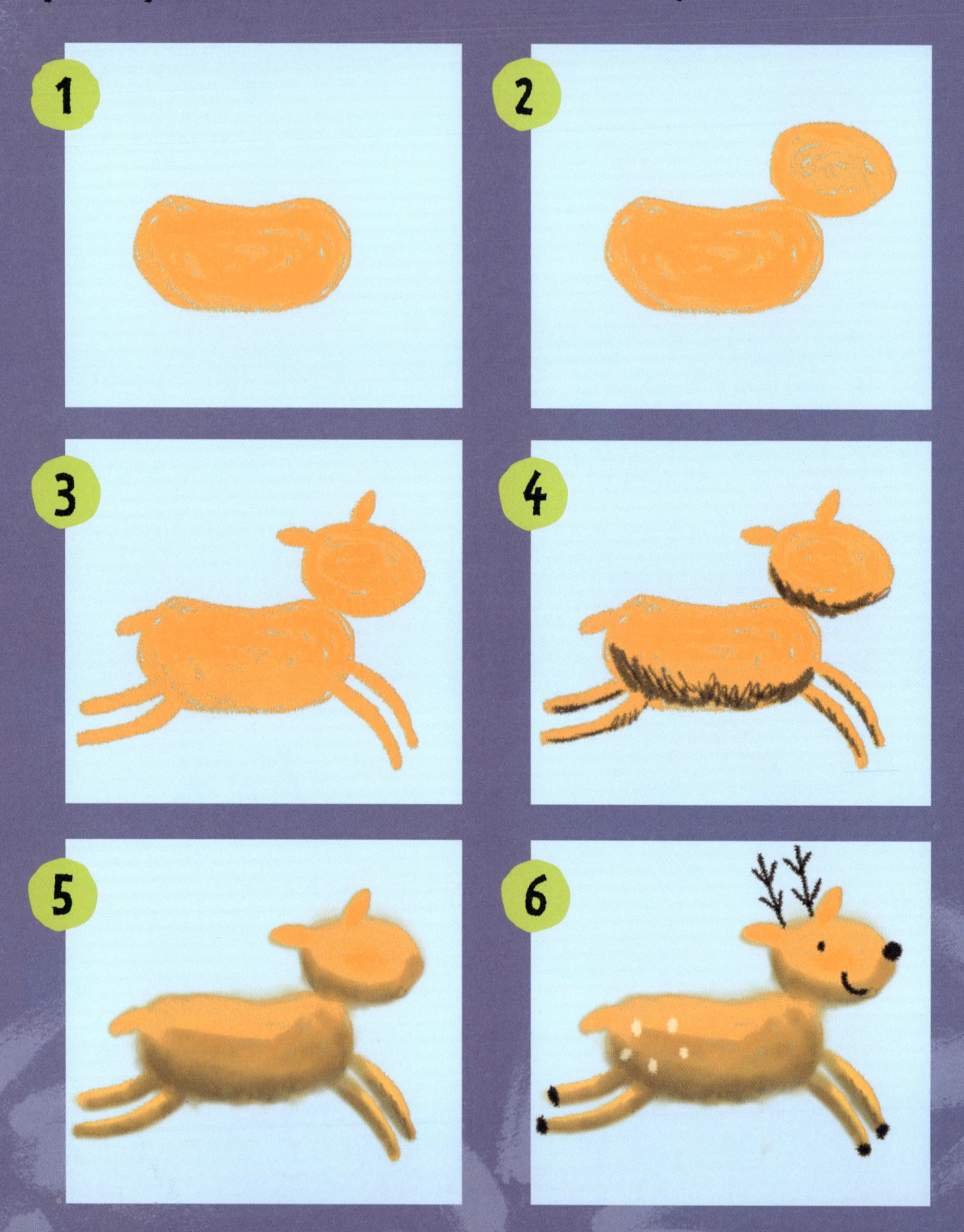

1
2
3
4
5
6

88

Santa needs more reindeer to pull his sleigh full of presents. Add some now!

FABULOUS FIREWORKS

Use curved lines, stars, and dots. Then smudge and add sparkles of chalk dust.

Oooh! Ahhh! Create a brilliant firework display to light up the sky!

HAUNTED HOUSE

Use white chalk side-on to create spooky shapes. Then add ghostly details!

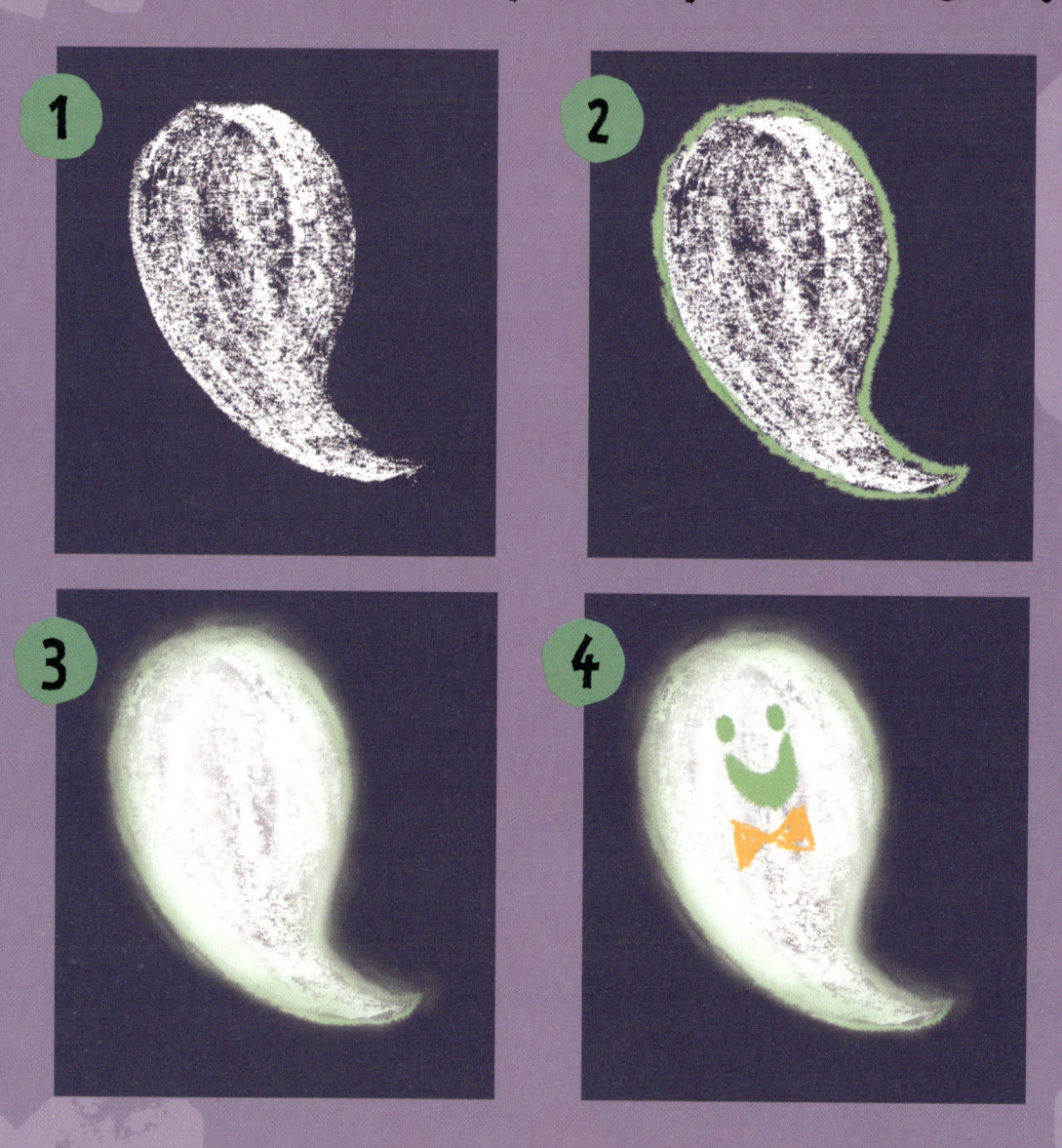

1
2
3
4

Eeek! Black chalk is perfect for making bat shapes.

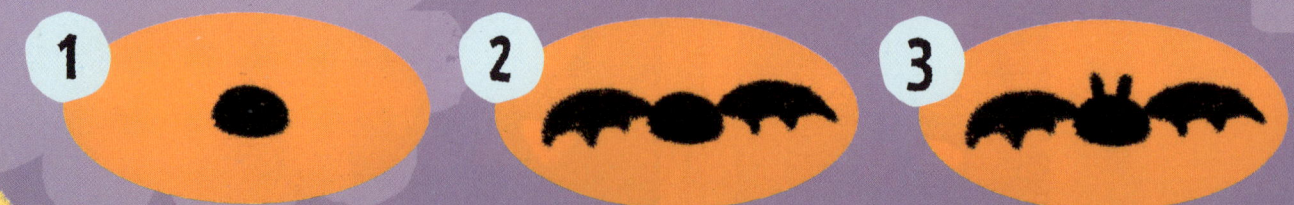

1
2
3

Add more ghosts and bats to make this haunted house extra-spooky!

WHOOSHING WITCHES

Start with a broom, then build up the witch to ride it. Smudge the end of the broomstick to give it some high-speed power!

1
2
3
4
5
6

Zoom! Fill the night sky with witches flying about on their broomsticks!

WONDERFUL WEATHER

Rain or shine? Can you draw these different types of weather?

96